MAGIC
BONE

TWO TALES, ONE DOG

For my parents, Steve and Gladys, who took me places, showed me the world, and taught me how important coming home again can be—NK

For James B—SB

GROSSET & DUNLAP
Penguin Young Readers Group
An Imprint of Penguin Random House LLC

The publisher does not have any control over and does not assume any responsibility for author or third-party websites or their content.

Text copyright © 2016 by Nancy Krulik. Illustrations copyright © 2016 by Sebastien Braun. All rights reserved. Published by Grosset & Dunlap, an imprint of Penguin Random House LLC, 345 Hudson Street, New York, New York 10014. GROSSET & DUNLAP is a trademark of Penguin Random House LLC. Printed in the USA.

Library of Congress Cataloging-in-Publication Data is available.

ISBN 9780448488776   10 9 8 7 6 5 4 3 2 1

MAGIC
BONE

TWO TALES, ONE DOG

by Nancy Krulik
illustrated by Sebastien Braun

Grosset & Dunlap
An Imprint of Penguin Random House

CHAPTER 1

"GRRRRRRR! GET THIS THING OFF OF ME!"

My eyes fly open. I leap onto my paws.

I was asleep. But that barking woke me right up!

"I said, GET THIS THING OFF OF ME!"

It's coming from my next-door neighbor, Frankie. He's a German shepherd. When he barks like that, the whole neighborhood can hear him.

What's going on?

I walk over to my fence and peer through the holes.

Frankie's two-leg is trying to take something off his back. It looks like a coat that is tied to a leash.

"Get this harness off of me!" Frankie sounds really mad.

Frankie's two-leg unstraps the coat-leash thing. She takes it inside.

"That's better," Frankie says, shaking his body. Then he spots me peeking through the fence. "What are you staring at, Sparky?"

"Nothing," I tell him. "I just wanted to say hi."

"Hi," Frankie grumbles back. "Did you see that awful thing? There is no way I am ever going for a walk with that harness on again. Ever."

"What's wrong with a harness?" I ask him.

"Are you nuts?" Frankie yells at me.

"No, I'm *Sparky*," I tell him. "Remember?"

Frankie frowns and grumbles something under his breath.

"I like when Josh and I go for a walk with my leash," I continue. "That way I know we'll stay together."

"Dogs are supposed to run free," Frankie tells me. "My two-leg is so slow. Sometimes I have to pull her just to get her moving."

"Sometimes I pull Josh, too," I admit. "And sometimes he pulls me. But the best time is when we walk side by side."

"Yeah, well, my two-leg can *never* keep up with me," Frankie says. "Now she's making me wear this ridiculous harness instead of a collar when we walk."

"Why does she do that?" I ask him.

"Why do two-legs do *anything*?" Frankie asks me.

I don't have an answer for that.

"I'm telling you, one day I'm going to break free of that thing," Frankie says. "Then I'm going to run and run and run. Like a dog is supposed to."

I do not think dogs are meant to run like that. What if I ran really far away, and Josh couldn't find me? That would be awful.

But I don't say that to Frankie. I don't think he is in the mood to

4

hear me argue with him.

Frankie lies down under the tree in his yard.

Snore. Snore. Snore.

Frankie isn't talking anymore. He's asleep.

Now I have no one to talk to.

Josh is not home. He went away in his metal machine with the four round paws.

So I have no one to play with, either.

I have nothing to do. Unless . . . Wait! I know something fun I can do all by myself. I can dig!

I race over to the place where Josh keeps his flowers. *Diggety, dig, dig.* Dirt flies everywhere. I am digging a really big hole. I am a great digger. *Diggety, dig . . .*

Hey. What's that in the middle of my hole?

It's a bone. *My* bone. My big, bright, sparkly bone.

"Hello, bone!" I bark.

The bone doesn't answer. Bones can't bark.

Sniffety, sniff, sniff. The bone smells so meaty. I just have to take a bite.

CHOMP!

Wiggle, waggle, whew. I feel dizzy—like my insides are spinning all around—but my outsides are standing still. Stars are twinkling in front of my eyes—even though it's daytime! All around me I smell food— fried chicken, salmon, roast beef. But there isn't any food in sight.

Kaboom! Kaboom! Kaboom!

CHAPTER 2

The *kabooming* stops.

I look around. I see trees.

But none of them are *my* tree!

I see rocks.

But I don't see my fence.

Or my house.

I don't know where I am, but I know where I am *not*. I'm not home anymore. I'm somewhere I've never been before.

How did I get here?

Then I remember the meaty-smelling bone I am holding between my teeth.

That's right! My bone *kaboomed* me to this place. It can do that because it is a magic bone! It can *kaboom* me *anywhere*!

The first time I took a bite of my magic bone, it took me all the way to London, England. London was fun—and *yummy, yum, yum*. Two-legs there drop all kinds of food: sausages, cheese, fish and *chips*. They're all just waiting for a dog like me to scoop them up!

Another time my bone *kaboomed* me to Paris, France. I got to dance around in puddles of paint, which was a lot of fun—even if the paint turned my paws purple.

I've been to a lot of different places with my magic bone. But the best place my bone takes me is home. Whenever I'm ready to leave a place, I just take a bite and my bone brings me right back to the house I share with Josh.

That is why I have to keep my magic bone safe. I do not want some other dog getting its teeth on it. I will need my bone when I am ready to leave this place.

Drip. Drip. Drip.

Wiggle, waggle, weird. It sounds like it's raining. But I don't feel any water on my fur.

I turn and look around.

Wiggle, waggle, weirder. Those rocks behind me are drooling water. Lots and lots of water. There's a big pool of rock drool underneath them.

Sometimes I drool when I'm hungry.

But I've never seen *rocks* drool before.

I think I'll bury my magic bone next to this big pile of drooling rocks. That will make it easy to find when I want to go home again.

I look around to make sure no one is watching where I bury my bone.

All I see are trees, bushes, flowers, and rocks. There's no one here but me.

So I start to dig.

Diggety, dig, dig. Dirt flies all around. I am making a big hole.

I drop my bone into the hole and *pushity, push, push* the dirt back over it. Now no one will be able to find my bone—except me, of course.

"What you got there?"

Uh-oh. There's someone else here. And that someone else is another dog. I can tell because she's speaking dog.

But I don't see the other dog. She must be hiding.

"Um . . . nothing," I say quickly.

Just then the other dog comes walking out from behind a big bush. She is all wet. There are leaves in her short brown-and-tan fur.

"You were pretty busy burying something," she says.

Gulp.

"Was it food?" she asks me.

I shake my head. "No. It was . . . nothing."

"Okay." She shrugs. "I'm not hungry, anyway. I just caught a giant fish and ate the whole thing."

Fish. *Yummy, yum, yum.* I love fish. Now I'm kind of hungry. And thirsty, too. All that digging is a lot of work.

I walk down to the pool of water below the drooling rocks. I start to lap up some water. *Slurp, slurp, slurp.*

Yum! The water is nice and cool. Which is great, because this place— whatever it's called—is really, really hot.

"I've never seen a dog like you before," the other dog says.

"I've never seen a dog like you before, either," I tell her.

"You haven't run into a pack of African wild dogs in the Serengeti before?" she asks, sounding surprised.

The Serengeti. That must be the name of this place.

"What kind of dog are you, anyway?" she asks me.

"I'm a sheepdog puppy," I tell her. "My name is Sparky."

"I'm Rehema," she says. Then she looks around. "Where's the rest of your pack?"

My pack? I don't have a pack. It's just me and Josh.

But I don't want to tell her about

Josh. I don't want to say that he went away for a little while in his metal machine with the four round paws and left me in our yard.

Because then she might ask me where my yard is. And how I got here.

I do not want to tell her about my magic bone.

"Don't worry," she says. "I won't tell anyone else that you've run away from your pack. I've run away from my pack, too. I do it all the time. Sometimes a dog's just got to run free, you know?"

"I guess," I say.

"I mean, I don't need some other dog telling me where to hunt. Or when to sleep, or . . ." Rehema keeps talking. I'm having a hard time keeping up with her. She talks really fast.

"If I want to catch my dinner in the morning, then I should be able to catch my dinner in the morning," Rehema continues. "And if I want to climb to the top of Mount Kilimanjaro, then I should be able to—"

"Mount Kili-what?" I interrupt her.

"Mount Kilimanjaro," Rehema repeats. "It's a mountain that's pretty far away from here. It is so tall, you can't see the top."

"Why would you want to climb that?" I ask her.

"I don't know." Rehema shrugs. "Because it's there, I guess. No one should tell me what I can or can't do. Like, right now, I want to swim. So I'm gonna swim."

The next thing I know, Rehema is in the big pool of water, paddling around.

"Come on in," she says. "The water is fine."

I shake my head. I like to put water in my inside. I don't like to feel it on my outside.

"Rehema! Rehema!" Another dog is calling Rehema's name.

"Who's that?" I ask.

Rehema paddles back to the land

and walks out of the water. "Shhh . . ." she whispers. "Be quiet. We don't want *him* to know we're here. Believe me."

She shoots me a look that tells me I better not ask any more questions. So I just stand there. I don't move. I don't speak.

"Rehema, let's go." The dog barks even louder. "Now!"

Gulp. That dog sounds really angry. And scary. So scary that I forget I'm supposed to be quiet.

"Why are we hiding?" I whisper to Rehema.

"Shhh . . . ," my new friend warns. "He'll hear us. African wild dogs have really good hearing."

That's no big deal. I have good hearing, too.

But I don't say that. I'm trying to *shhh*.

Just then a brown, black, and tan dog peers through the bushes. He is much bigger than Rehema and me, and he does not look happy.

"The pack is back from the hunt, Rehema," he growls. "So we've got food—no thanks to you."

"I already ate," Rehema tells him. "I caught a fish."

"*I'm* hungry," I say.

The big dog looks at me. "Who's this?" he asks Rehema.

"I'm Sparky," I tell him.

"He's a stranger," the big dog says.

"He's my friend," Rehema insists.

"He's not one of our pack," the big dog tells her.

"He's a dog," Rehema says. "And he's nice."

"He's a different *kind* of dog," the other dog grumbles.

"We're all different, Amiri," Rehema says. "You have brown and black spots. I have brown and tan spots. Sparky's practically all white. So what?"

Amiri shakes his head. "You know how risky it is to be around someone who isn't in the pack," he says. "The Serengeti is filled with dangerous characters."

"I'm not dangerous," I tell him.

"Where's *your* pack?" Amiri asks me.

"At home," I say.

"He's alone." Rehema smiles at me.

Grumble rumble. That's the sound of my tummy telling me that it's hungry.

"Sounds like you could use some food," Rehema says. "Let's go have dinner."

"Oh brother," Amiri says. "Another mouth to feed. Just what we need."

CHAPTER 3

There's not much meat left when we get back to Rehema's pack.

"Take mine," Rehema offers. "I already ate. You guys should have seen the fish I caught. It was this big!" She spreads her paws wide on the ground.

"Sure, Rehema," a dog with small black spots on her back says.

"I mean it, Zahra," Rehema tells the dog. "You guys should go on

adventures sometime. You would be surprised what food you can catch. Like, I remember one time . . ."

"Here she goes again," Amiri growls.

Rehema shoots him an angry look. Then she smiles at me.

"It was when I was climbing Mount Kilimanjaro," she tells me. "This hornbill came flying over my head. I leaped up in the air and caught it in my bare paws."

The other dogs in the pack stare at her.

"That's pretty high," one of them says. "I mean, birds can fly, and dogs don't have wings or—"

"I caught it, Mahir," Rehema insists.

"That's amazing," I say. "I never met any dog who could jump that high before."

"You still haven't met one," Zahra says. "Rehema is always telling stories, but they're never true."

"Remember that time she said she fought off a lion with her bare paws?" Amiri says. He starts to laugh.

Rehema's eyes grow small and angry. "Go ahead and laugh. But I bet none of you ever did that."

"Neither did you," Zahra insists.

Rehema gives Zahra a dirty look. But she smiles at me. "You should have seen that lion, Sparky," she says. "He was huge. His fangs were dripping. He wanted to eat me."

Gulp. I don't know what a lion is. But I wouldn't want to be near anything that wanted to eat me.

"You didn't run away?" I ask her.

"Nope," Rehema says proudly. "I bit him on the back. Then I wrestled him to the ground. He didn't bother me after that."

Zahra laughs loudly.

"You'd be better off spending your time helping us hunt than making up stories," Amiri tells Rehema angrily. "Especially if you're going to bring friends here to share in *our* catch."

He gives me a dirty look.

"Imagine how much more food we could have had if you all had tried a different giant water puddle to fish in," Rehema says. "You guys never want to do anything new."

"Our usual water puddle is pretty big," Mahir says. "And it has fish."

"It doesn't have giant fish like the one I caught this morning," Rehema tells him.

"Stop, Rehema," Amiri barks at her. "We all know you didn't catch anything."

"That does it!" Rehema growls angrily. "I'm out of here. I'll show you all."

With that, Rehema takes off. She runs faster than any dog I've ever seen.

I could never catch up with her.

Which means I'm stuck here with a bunch of dogs I don't know.

And who don't seem very friendly.

At least not to me.

"Rehema!" I call out to her. "Come back."

Zahra shakes her head. "Don't worry. She'll come back in a little while."

"It just means more food for us," Amiri adds. He takes another bite of meat.

Well . . . that is true. I open my mouth to take another bite, too. But Amiri grabs it out from under me.

"I said for *us*," Amiri tells me. "Our pack."

"You're not part of our pack," Zahra says. She looks me up and down like she's seeing me for the first time. "You're not even an African wild dog."

Boy, these dogs are mean. I think maybe I will just get my bone and go home.

I turn around to head back to the drooling rocks. But before I can even take a step—

ROAR!

Wiggle, waggle, what was that?

CHAPTER 4

ROAR!

There it is again.

That sound is really loud.

My whole body starts to shake.

I'm scared.

And I'm not the only one.

"Uh-oh." Mahir gulps.

"They're back," Zahra adds.

"Who's back?" I ask her.

"The lions." Zahra points her snout in the direction of a big pile of giant rocks.

That's when I see a cat with fluffy fur all around his face. He's the biggest cat I've ever seen. A lot bigger than Queenie, the cat who lives in my neighborhood.

ROAR!

Gulp. He's a lot louder than Queenie, too.

There are other giant cats on the rock. One of them opens her mouth and licks her lips.

Gulp. Again.

Those are some big, sharp cat teeth.

My tail tucks itself between my legs. It doesn't like the look of those teeth.

Neither do I.

"Should we warn Rehema that the

lions are around?" Mahir asks Amiri.

"*I* think we should," I say before Amiri can answer. "Those cats might want to steal Rehema's food."

"No, they won't," Zahra says with a nasty laugh.

Phew.

"They'll want to eat *her*," Zahra continues.

Yikes. Giant cats who eat dogs? What kind of place is this Serengeti?

The kind of place I want to leave. Right now. Except . . .

My magic bone is buried over by the rocks that drool water. If I want to get to it, I have to go past the giant lion cats that eat dogs.

That doesn't sound like such a great idea.

"We *have* to warn her," Amiri says. "It's the rule of the pack. One for all and all for one. African wild dogs take care of one another."

"Even though she's the one who took off?" Zahra argues.

"It doesn't matter," Amiri says firmly. "Remember that time you had a sick stomach?"

"I remember," Mahir butts in. He looks at me. "It was really gross, Sparky. Zahra couldn't take two steps without having to stop and—"

"It wasn't my fault," Zahra interrupts. "I was sick."

"And who made sure you had a tasty lizard to eat when you felt better?" Amiri asks her.

Zahra frowns. "Rehema."

"Exactly," Amiri says. "She took care of you. We take care of one another. And that's why we have to warn her."

"Rehema! Come back," Mahir begins to shout.

"The lions are out on the hunt!" Zahra adds.

I wait and listen for Rehema to answer. But I don't hear anything.

"Maybe she's hiding," I suggest.

"She could be," Mahir agrees. "Rehema is smart. She won't do anything to let the lions know where she is."

"Rehema *is* smart," Amiri says. "But she's also reckless. It's hard to protect yourself when you're all alone. We must go look for her."

ROAR!

I can still hear the lions as we hurry off to find Rehema.

ROAR!

Those lions sure sound hungry.

I hope Rehema really is just hiding.

Because if she isn't, she could be in real trouble.

And I don't want to think about *that.*

CHAPTER 5

My paws are tired. My belly is empty. And my tongue is very, very thirsty. There's a giant water bowl just ahead. A bowl that's so big, I can't see the other side.

I want to stop and have a drink.

But the African wild dogs aren't stopping at the giant water bowl. So I can't stop. I have to stay with the pack.

GRUNT! GROAN! ROAR!

"Aaahhhh!" I shout. "What was that? Did the lions follow us?"

The other dogs start laughing.

I don't understand. There's nothing funny about all that grunting. Or groaning. Or roaring.

GRUNT! GROAN! ROAR!

"We have to get out of here!" I shout. I run and hide behind a big bush.

But the other dogs don't move. They just stand there, laughing.

"Come on! We're gonna get eaten!" I warn them.

"No, we're not," Zahra says. "Hippos don't eat dogs."

"What-os?" I ask her.

"Hippos," Mahir repeats. He points his snout toward the giant water bowl. "See? They're playing in that giant water puddle."

I peer out from behind the bushes

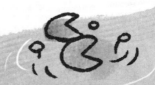

and look at the giant water bowl that is so big I can't see the other side.

Wiggle, waggle, whoa! Those are the biggest four-legs I have ever seen! They are brownish gray, and they have hardly any fur.

Some of the giant four-legs are paddling around in the water.

Some are resting in the mud.

But none of them are trying to eat the African wild dogs.

"They don't *eat* dogs," Amiri explains. "But it's still never a great idea to go near them."

"Look at their size. If they wanted to, they could crush you," Zahra says. She gives me a nasty grin.

I get the feeling she wouldn't mind watching me get crushed.

"Those hippos make me laugh," Mahir says. "Look how they roll around in the mud."

Mahir gets down on the ground and starts rolling around.

"Hey, this is pretty fun," he says. "The ground is nice and cool."

"Let me try," Zahra says.

She gets down on the ground and

rolls over and over.

The next thing I know, Amiri is on his back, scratching back and forth in the dirt.

"African wild dogs do everything together," he says. Then he rolls onto his belly and licks Zahra on the nose.

Zahra laughs. Her tail wags.

That's the happiest I've seen Zahra all day.

Mahir wiggles his belly in the dirt. He is laughing, too.

"We're hippos!" he barks happily.

They sure look like they are having fun.

"I want to try!" I shout. I drop to the ground—

ROAR!

Uh-oh.

That didn't sound like hippos having fun in the mud.

It sounded more like a cat.

Not a little, meowing, hissing cat.

A big, roaring, angry cat.

"D-d-did you hear that?" I ask the African wild dogs.

Amiri stands still. His ears are stiff.

ROAR!

"That lion must have picked up our scent," Amiri says. "He followed us. We gotta go. NOW."

"You can say that again," Zahra says.

"Why?" Mahir asks her. "Didn't you hear him the first time?"

Zahra doesn't answer. She just hurries off behind Amiri.

Mahir races right after her.

The African wild dogs may act brave when they're near the hippos.

But they're not so brave when it comes to lions.

ROAR!

Neither am I.

"Hey, you guys!" I shout. "Wait for me!"

CHAPTER 6

My paws keep on running. Fast. Faster. *Fastest.*

They're moving so fast, they *zoomity, zoom, zoom* right past the African wild dogs!

My paws are really scared of that lion.

"Hey, wait up," Amiri orders.

He hurries to catch up to me. So do Mahir and Zahra.

"You can't run faster than the rest of us," Amiri scolds me.

"Yes, he can," Mahir says. "He just did."

Zahra kicks him in the rear.

"That's not what Amiri meant," she says. "He meant that in the Serengeti, you gotta follow the rules."

"And the rule is, we travel in a pack," Amiri tells me. "It's safer that way. Because the bigger the pack, the scarier we seem."

"I don't think this fluffy guy will scare anyone." Zahra sniffs in my direction.

I like my fluffy fur.

I do *not* like Zahra.

"Maybe you can learn to hunt," Amiri tells me. "We can use another hunter in the pack. Especially since Rehema's only interested in catching food for herself these days."

I stop to *thinkety, think, think* about that.

I know the other dogs were being mean to Rehema. It wasn't nice that they didn't believe her when she said she caught a fish.

But what if she did catch the fish? And ate it all by herself?

That's not nice, either. She should share her food with the pack. Just like they share their food with her.

I don't know who is right and who is wrong.

Living in a big pack sure is complicated.

Amiri looks up at the sky. "It's going to be dark in a little while," he says. "If we don't find Rehema, she'll be out there alone. We can't let that happen."

Dark. I don't like dark. It's scary in the dark. That's why I like to cuddle up with Josh in his great big two-leg bed when it's dark in our house.

JOSH!

He's probably going to be home soon, and I won't be there.

I can't let that happen. I have to go back to the rocks that drool water. I have to dig up my bone. I have to *kaboom* home!

But I can't go to the drooling rocks by myself. I can't leave the pack.

And the pack won't go back until they find Rehema.

Which means we have to find her fast.

But she could be anywhere. Back near those trees. Or by the rocks over there. Or by that big mountain . . .

"That's it!" I shout.

"What's it?" Zahra asks me.

"I bet Rehema went to climb Mount Kilimahooziwhatsit."

"Mount what?" Mahir asks.

"I think Sparky means Mount Kilimanjaro," Amiri says. Then he shakes his head. "No, she wouldn't be there."

"She could be," I insist. "She talked a lot about climbing that mountain. She wants to reach the top of it."

"Do you have any idea how far Mount Kilimanjaro is from here?"

Zahra asks me. "Or how high it is? What dog would want to climb all the way up there?"

"Rehema," I tell her.

"Why would she want to do that?" Zahra asks.

I know the answer to that one. "Because it's there," I answer.

"That's silly," Mahir says.

Now I'm getting mad. I don't think the African wild dogs really want to find Rehema. They just want to complain about her.

"Do you have a better idea?" I ask them angrily.

They don't answer me.

"Well, I'm going to start walking toward that mountain," I tell them. "Are you coming with me?"

Amiri, Zahra, and Mahir all stare at me. I think they are surprised at how brave I sound.

I'm surprised at how brave I sound. Because I don't feel brave. I just sound that way. Inside I'm kind of scared.

I wonder if Rehema sounds braver than she really is, too. I wonder if she's scared out there all alone without her pack.

"Sure, we're coming," Amiri finally agrees. "Like we told you. In a pack, it's all for one and one for all."

Phew. That's good. I didn't want to go to the big, scary mountain all by myself. Also, I'm not sure which way to go or how I'm going to find it. But I'm sure the African wild dogs know where the mountain is.

"Let's go," I say.

But before I can take another step, the ground begins to shake underneath me.

I hear pawsteps. Lots and lots of pawsteps.

THUMP BUMP. THUMP BUMP.

What's going on?

Lub dub. Lub dub.

That's my heart. It's pounding almost as loud and strong as the pawsteps.

THUMP BUMP. THUMP BUMP.

They're coming right for us.

Slowly, I turn around and . . .

AAAHHH!!!

CHAPTER 7

All I see are legs.

Gray furry legs.

Black furry legs.

Brown furry legs.

Striped furry legs.

There are big four-legs. And little four-legs.

And they are all running together in a big giant pack!

THUMP BUMP. THUMP BUMP. THUMP BUMP.

The ground all around me is thumping and bumping. Even the trees are shaking!

I've never felt anything like this before.

"What's happening?" I ask the African wild dogs.

But they don't answer.

That's because they're not there. They've disappeared.

"Get out of the way!" I hear Amiri's voice coming from the bushes.

"They'll stomp right over you," Mahir adds.

"Those wildebeests don't stop for anyone!" Zahra says.

I don't know what a wilde-whatsit is. But there's no time to find out. I zoom over to the bushes where the wild dogs are hiding.

Lub dub. Lub dub.

My heart is pounding.

Heh. Heh. Heh.

My mouth is panting.

"What. Is. Going. On?" I ask the dogs, in between pants.

"The wildebeests are on the move," Mahir tells me.

"The what?" I ask.

"Wildebeests," Mahir repeats. "Those gray and black four-legs with the big horns."

"Where are they going?" I ask him.

"I don't know," Mahir admits.

"Where are the other four-legs going?" I wonder.

"You mean the zebras and the gazelles?" Mahir asks.

I nod. I guess that's what I mean. I'm not really sure.

"They're going wherever the wildebeests are going," Mahir tells me.

"Do you think Rehema is traveling with them, too?" I ask.

"I doubt it," Amiri says.

"Why would she leave a pack of dogs to run off with those characters?" Zahra asks me.

"Maybe she was looking for something different," I say.

The African wild dogs stare at me. They don't know what to say. I've stumped them!

THUMP BUMP. BUMP THUMP.

The ground keeps shaking as all those four-legs thunder by.

"Looks like someone's chasing down dinner," Zahra says. She looks toward a big spotted cat running behind the crowd. "That cheetah is going to grab the first wildebeest to get tired."

"Why would that big cat want to hurt the wildebeests?" I ask as the giant cat races past us.

"Why do you think?" Amiri sounds annoyed. "Because she's a cheetah. That's what cheetahs do."

Amiri doesn't have to be so mean. It's not my fault I've never been to a place where the cats are so big and dangerous before.

The African wild dogs and I stand for a while in the bushes, watching as the big crowd of four-legs runs past us.

The ground shakes under our paws.

THUMP BUMP.

THUMP BUMP.

And then—suddenly—the thumping and bumping stops.

Just like that.

It's quiet. And calm.

"Come on," I say to the African

wild dogs. "We can start looking for Rehema again."

I walk out of the bushes and start heading toward the giant mountain.

But no one else's paws are moving.

"Come on, you guys!" I shout to the African wild dogs. "Why are you still hiding in those bushes?"

THUMP BUMP! THUMP BUMP!

The African wild dogs don't answer me.

That's probably because they can't hear me over all that *THUMP-BUMPING.*

There's a whole new crowd of gray, black, and white four-legs running this way.

And coming up behind them is an orange and black-spotted cat.

It's another cheetah!

Her paws are moving *fast, faster, fastest.*

She's racing right toward me. *And her mouth is wide open.*

"Run, paws!" I shout to my paws. "Run! Now!"

But my paws don't run.

They are frozen stiff, like the ice statues I saw in Zermatt, Switzerland.

I can't move.

Any second now that cheetah is going to gobble me up!

CHAPTER 8

OOOOMF!

Something—or *someone*—shoves me. Hard. Right in my side.

Wiggle, waggle, WHOA!

I am flying through the air. Kind of like a bird. Except I don't have any wings.

THUD!

I land on my rear end. That hurt!

Zahra comes running over.

"Are you an idiot?" she barks in my face.

"N-no," I answer. "I'm a sheepdog."

Zahra rolls her eyes and breathes heavily. Amiri and Mahir race over to us.

"Why did you run out into the stampede like that?" Mahir asks Zahra. "You could have been killed."

Zahra shrugs. "I saw Sparky standing there, like cheetah bait. The next thing I knew, I was pushing him out of the way. I didn't think about it. I just did it."

"You did it because he's a dog, and dogs help one another," Amiri says. "You saved his life. I'm proud of you."

Zahra gives me a dirty look. "Um . . . You're *welcome*," she says nastily.

Oops. I was so scared that I forgot my manners.

"Thank you for saving my life," I tell her. And I mean it.

"No problem," Zahra answers. She starts walking toward a giant water bowl near some huge rocks. "I need a drink of water. All this life-saving stuff has made me thirsty."

"Come on." Amiri follows her.

But before we can lap up one drop of water, I see something.

"Uh-oh," I say. "There's someone in the water."

"Who is it?" Zahra asks. She sounds worried.

"I don't know," I say. "All I see is a tail."

"You think it's someone friendly?" Zahra asks Amiri.

"Or someone who wants to eat us?" Mahir asks nervously.

That makes *me* nervous.

Before Amiri can answer, the four-leg pops her head out of the water. She's got a big fish between her teeth.

"It's Rehema!" I shout excitedly.

Amiri, Mahir, and Zahra all stare at Rehema. Then they stare at the fish.

"She was telling the truth," Zahra says slowly. "That fish is huge."

"Wow," Amiri murmurs. He seems really surprised.

"Dinnertime!" Mahir shouts. He hurries over to Rehema.

We all follow close behind. A moment later we are standing by the big rocks near the water bowl.

There are little rocks beneath my paws. They are hard to walk on.

"Hi, you guys!" Rehema barks to us.

It is a little hard to understand her, because she has the fish between her teeth.

"Look what I got for us," she adds

proudly. "I told you I could catch a giant fish. And this isn't even the biggest one. You should have seen the one that got away. It—"

Rehema doesn't get to finish what she is saying. At just that moment, Amiri spots something high up on one of the nearby rocks.

"Hey," he whispers nervously. "Don't look now. But we've got company."

CHAPTER 9

Usually I like company. When company comes to our house, I jump up and lick them on their faces.

Josh has nice friends. I like when they are our company.

But that's not the kind of company Amiri is talking about.

This company isn't someone you play with.

This company is a big scary lion.

His tongue is licking his teeth.

I can't tell if he wants to eat our fish—or if he wants to eat *us*.

Wiggle, waggle, what are we going to do now?

"This is your chance, Rehema," Amiri says. "Why don't you go wrestle that lion with your bare paws?"

"Wh-what?" Rehema asks him nervously. "You want me to *fight* him?"

"You're always bragging about how you once wrestled a lion," Zahra reminds her.

"Yeah, well, about that . . . ," Rehema says slowly. "Maybe I exaggerated a teensy bit."

"Really? What a surprise," Zahra says. Except she doesn't sound surprised at all.

"I'll bet you never caught a

hornbill in midair either, huh?"

"Well," Rehema admits, "I ate a hornbill *egg* once. I took it out of the nest while the mother bird was away."

"Guys, I hate to break up the conversation," Mahir says. "But what are we going to do? That lion is definitely going to spot us soon."

"We could leave him the fish and run," Zahra suggests.

"What?" Rehema says. "No way. Do you have any idea how hard I worked to get this fish for us?"

"I don't think he'll be satisfied with a fish if he can eat five dogs," Amiri says.

My tail tucks itself far between my legs. It's scared. And so am I.

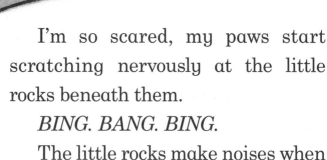

I'm so scared, my paws start scratching nervously at the little rocks beneath them.

BING. BANG. BING.

The little rocks make noises when they hit the big rock behind me.

The lion looks around. He opens his mouth.

YIKES! His teeth look sharp.

My paws scratch harder at the little rocks. They're scared of those teeth. Which is kind of weird, since paws can't see.

Scratch. Scratch. Scratch.
CLINK. CLANG. CLUNK.

The little rocks hit the big rock again.

The lion stands very still. His body gets stiff.

He looks scared.

Could it be? Is that big giant cat scared of the noise little rocks make when they hit a big rock?

I scratch at the little rocks again. They go flying all around.

PLINK. PLUNK. PLONK.

At the sound of the little rocks hitting the big rock, the lion starts to back up.

That's it!

"The lion is scared of the noise!" I tell the others. "Everybody start scratching!"

The African wild dogs stare at me.

"What?" Mahir asks.

"I can't imagine a big lion being scared of some rock noises," Amiri tells me.

"I can't, either," I admit. "But it looks like he is."

"It's worth a try," Rehema says. She starts to paw at the rocks.

Clink. Plink. BONK.

The lion listens for a minute.

He backs up a little farther.

"It's working!" I shout. "Come on. Let's make it louder."

The African wild dogs and I scratch at the rocks with our paws. We scratch really, really hard.

Scratch. Scratch. SCRATCH.
CLINK. CLANK. CLONK.
FLINK. FLANK. FLONK.

That rock sounds really loud now.

The lion turns around and runs as fast as he can.

"Sparky!" Rehema shouts out excitedly. "You did it! You saved us all!"

"I didn't save us," I tell Rehema.

"Sure you did," Rehema insists. "The lion is gone, isn't he?"

"We all made the noise," I say. "One dog couldn't have made a noise loud enough to scare off a lion. You need a whole pack working together."

"We do work pretty well together," Zahra agrees.

"Hunting in packs makes sense,"

Amiri says. "It's safer, and we catch the food much more easily."

"But you guys always want to hunt in the same places," Rehema argues.

"So?" Zahra asks.

"Look at this fish I caught in the giant water puddle," Rehema says. "We never would have gotten one this big in our usual puddle. They don't get that big there."

"That's true," Zahra admits.

"You guys didn't believe me when I told you I could catch bigger fish," Rehema says angrily.

"That's because nothing else you told us was the truth," Amiri insists.

"I only made up those stories because everything we do is so boring," Rehema says. "I have to use my imagination to make life more exciting."

I give her a funny look. With all these big cats, fat hippos, and running wildebeests, the Serengeti seems pretty exciting to me.

But I guess it's different if you live here all the time.

"That's not an excuse for lying," Amiri tells her.

"I guess not," Rehema admits. "But we really should try new places to hunt. And maybe have a little fun."

"That is an awfully big fish," Mahir says slowly. "I'd like to try fishing in this water for a change."

"Me too," Zahra says.

Amiri nods. "I agree. It might be fun to go on some new adventures *together*."

Rehema smiles. "Imagine all the food we can catch now that we're a bigger pack."

Now I'm confused.

"A bigger pack?" I ask her.

"Sure," Rehema tells me. "With you, we are five."

Me? Oh no.

"I can't stay here," I tell her.

"I have to go home."

"At least wait until morning," Amiri says. "It will be easier to find your way."

I do not want to wait. I want to go home now.

"Rehema, how do I get back to the big rocks that drool water?" I ask.

Rehema gives me a funny look. "The big rocks that . . . ? Oh, you mean the waterfall," she says. "Where we met this morning."

I nod.

"That's a long walk," she says. "You have to go all the way around to the other side of this big water puddle."

I look at the giant puddle. It's so big, I can barely see the other side.

I can't swim that far.

Just then I spot something big and fat with brown-and-gray skin. He is swimming in the water.

It's a hippo.

He looks like he's a really good swimmer.

And that gives me an idea!

CHAPTER 10

Slowly, I go into the water. My back paws paddle. My front paws paddle.

Paddling is hard work. But I can't stop. Not until I reach the hippo playing in the water.

I'm scared of the hippo. But I can't let that stop me. I have to get back to my magic bone, and this hippo is my ride.

Quickly, I climb up past the hippo's small tail and high over his big hippo rear end. Now I am riding on his back.

The hippo is not happy to have me on his back. He tips to one side. Then he tips to the other. He is trying to throw me off.

"Hold on to his tail, Sparky!" Rehema shouts to me. "It's harder for him to toss you off if you hold on."

So I hold on. Finally the hippo gives up trying to throw me off. He goes back to swimming.

As the hippo swims, I call out to my new friends.

"Good-bye!" I shout.

"Good-bye!" I hear them bark back.

My tail waves good-bye. Well, it's wagging, anyway.

My tail is happy.

I guess that's because it knows we are going home!

Hooray! I can see the drooling rocks! I am back where I buried my bone!

As soon as the hippo reaches the shore, I leap off his back. Then I run. Fast. I do not want the hippo to catch me on land. He could squash me there.

But the hippo does not squash me. I think he is just happy to have me off his back. He turns around and swims away.

I race over to where I buried my bone. I start to *diggety, dig, dig.*

I am digging very fast. I want to get my bone and go back home, where the cats are small. And they do not want to eat dogs.

I want to go home to Josh!

Diggety, dig, dig. Diggety, dig . . .

There it is! My magic bone! Right in the middle of a big hole in the dirt.

All I have to do now is take a bite and . . .

Gulp!

Wiggle, waggle . . . What are those?

I see two massive gray four-legs. One is bigger than the other. But they both have huge ears, giant paws, and

the longest noses I have ever seen.

Quickly, I run away. I hide behind two giant rocks. The big-eared four-legs will never find me here.

Uh-oh. I ran away so fast, I left my magic bone in the middle of the big hole.

What if one of those big four-legs steals it? I'll be stuck in the Serengeti forever.

I want to go out there and grab my bone. But I can't.

Ohhhh . . . this is *baddy, bad, bad.*

The two big-eared, long-nosed four-legs keep on walking. They go right past where I am hiding. Right past the rocks that drool water. And right over the hole where my bone is sitting.

Crunch.

Oh no! I think one of the giant four-legs just stepped right on my magic bone.

I hold my breath and wait while the giant four-legs walk away. Then I run out from my hiding place. I need to check on my bone.

I look down. There's a crack right in the middle of my bone. But it's not broken all the way through.

I bend down and pick up the bone with my teeth. Then I bite down.

CHOMP!

Wiggle, waggle, whew. I feel dizzy—like my insides are spinning all around—but my outsides are standing still. Stars are twinkling in front of my eyes—even though it's daytime! All around me I smell food—fried chicken, salmon, roast beef. But there isn't any food in sight.

Kaboom! Kaboom! Kaboom!

CHAPTER 11

Hey! Where's my tree?

Where's my fence?

Where's my house?

WHERE AM I?

That big-eared four-leg must have done something terrible to my magic bone when he stepped on it and cracked it. Because my bone did not *kaboom* me home.

It kaboomed me somewhere I've never been before.

Somewhere where there are lots and lots *and lots* of two-legs. Big two-legs. Little two-legs. Thin two-legs. Fat two-legs.

But none of them are *my* two-leg. *I want my Josh!*

Wiggle, waggle, wait a minute. What's that coming down the road?

It's a four-leg. She's all by herself.

But it's not a dog four-leg. Or a cat four-leg. Or even a squirrel four-leg.

It's a *cow.* And she's walking right down the middle of the road!

The two-legs move to the side.

The metal machines with four big round paws stand still and let her pass.

Everything stops so that the cow can go by.

I've seen cows before, when my magic bone *kaboomed* me to a rodeo in Texas. But this cow isn't in a big ring. She's in the middle of the road.

What kind of a place is this?

A crowded place. That's what kind. A place filled with spicy smells my nose has never smelled before.

And a *hot* place. My whole body is hot. Even my tongue. It just popped out of my mouth to get some air!

Grumble rumble.

My tummy is hungry. So am I.

I didn't get to eat any of that big fish Rehema caught in the Serengeti.

I will search for a snack. But first, I'm going to bury my bone. It may not have worked the way I wanted it to, but it's still my only chance at getting back to Josh.

Maybe all my magic bone needs is a rest. I always do my tricks better when I am not so tired.

Grumble rumble. Or hungry. Like I am now.

I carry my bone over to a small patch of grass near a little tree at the side of the road. Then I start to *diggety, dig, dig.* Dirt flies everywhere.

There are lots of two-legs around,

but they don't even look at me. They just keep walking.

Diggety, dig, dig. I have made a nice big hole.

I drop my bone into the hole. Then I *pushity, push, push* some dirt right over it. Now no other dog will be able to find it.

If there are any other dogs in this place.

So far, all I've seen are two-legs, cows, and metal machines with big round paws.

A large crowd of two-legs goes running by.

"Ouch!" One of the two-legs steps on my paw. That hurt.

The two-leg doesn't stop to see if I am okay. I don't think he even

realizes that he stepped on me.

I don't like this place. I want to go home.

I want to sleep under my tree.

And dig near the flowers.

And cuddle with Josh.

But I can't. I'm stuck here with my broken magic bone.

What if my bone never works again?

What if I never see Josh again?

Oh, this is bad.

Baddy, bad, bad.

CHAPTER 12

Sniffety, sniff, sniff.

Just then, my nose smells something spicy. And meaty.

I do not want to think about scary, *baddy, bad, bad* things anymore.

Meat is not scary. Or bad.

Meat is *yummy, yum, yum.*

The meaty smell is coming from where all the two-legs are walking. Maybe one of them will drop a nice hunk of spicy meat onto the ground. Then I can eat it.

Sniffety, sniff, sniff.

Boo. No one is dropping any food.

Sniffety, sniff, sniff . . .

Hey, what's that?

Right in the middle of my sniffing, I spy something lying on the ground. It's not food. It looks like some sort of doggie chew toy.

A chew toy isn't as good as meat. But it will give my teeth something to chomp on while I look for food.

I pick up the chew toy with my mouth.

The toy is hard, and it doesn't make a loud squeaky noise like my toys at home do. But I can still chew on it.

Chew. Chew. Chew.

"Hey! Put that down!"

A dog leaps out from the crowd. He glares at me and bares his fangs. He is one angry dog!

"Do you have naan in your ears?" the angry dog asks me.

"Do I have what in my ears?" I ask. But I do not let go of the chew toy.

"Naan. Bread," he answers.

"Why would I have bread in my ears?" I ask him. "Bread goes in your tummy."

"Well, you must not have heard me," the angry dog says. "Because you're still holding that magic lamp."

"Do you mean this chew toy?" I ask him.

"That's not a chew toy," he says. "That's a magic lamp."

Huh? I've heard of a magic bone. But I've never heard of a magic lamp.

"What's so magical about it?" I ask the mixed-breed.

"Are you kidding?" he says. "You don't know about the jinni?"

"The what?" I wonder out loud.

"The jinni," the mixed-breed

repeats. "He's trapped inside the lamp."

I can't tell if this dog is telling me the truth or not.

"Someone lives inside this thing?" I ask him.

"A jinni," he says. "And if you set him free, he will give you anything you wish for."

"Anything?" I repeat.

The mixed-breed nods. "But you only get to wish for three things. And you can't wish for more wishes."

The chew toy in my mouth is really small. I can't imagine anyone fitting inside.

"How do you know there's a jinni living in *this* lamp?" I ask him. "Aren't there a lot of lamps around here?"

"Sure," the mixed-breed agrees. "But that lamp was right outside the Mankameshwar Temple." He points to a building near where I found the chew toy. "Everyone knows that wishes are granted there."

Not everyone knows that. *I* didn't know that. But now that I do, there's no way I'm giving up this chew toy—I mean, lamp.

Because if there really is a jinni inside, I can wish for him to send me home.

I drop the chew toy on the ground and start pawing at it. I am trying to open it up and see what is inside.

Paw, paw, paw. Paw, paw . . .

Pop! The top pops off the chew toy.

But no one comes out.

I look inside. There's nothing in there.

"There's nobody living in this chew toy," I tell the mixed-breed.

"Maybe he's an invisible jinni," the mixed-breed says.

"An inviz—?"

"Invisible," he repeats. "It means you can't see him, but he's there. And you just set him free."

"Which means I can wish for anything I want," I say.

"Yup," the mixed-breed grumbles. "Lucky you."

The mixed-breed doesn't sound very happy about my luck. I guess he wanted the jinni to grant *his* wishes instead of mine.

If there really is such a thing as an invisible jinni.

Maybe this dog is just teasing me.

Or maybe he's not.

I just don't know.

GRUMBLE RUMBLE.

My tummy sounds angry. It

doesn't care about the jinni. It just cares about food.

"I'm sorry, tummy," I say. "I wish I had some food to give you."

Just then a two-leg passes by, eating as he walks.

PLOP.

The two-leg drops a big hunk of chicken and some fried bread right at my paws.

Wow!

"See?" the mixed-breed says. "The jinni made your wish come true."

"I never saw any bread like this before," I say. "Is it yummy?"

"The samosa? Sure, it's yummy," the mixed-breed tells me. "Of course, I would have wished for something a whole lot better if *I'd* been the one to free the jinni."

Chomp! I take a big bite of the chicken.

Owie! Wowie! "That's really spicy!" I exclaim.

"Take a bite of the samosa," the mixed-breed says. "It's not spicy at all. It will make your mouth feel better."

I bite off a piece of the fried bread. *Yummy, yum, yum.* There's potato inside.

"You mind if I finish the chicken?" the mixed-breed asks me. "I like spicy curry."

"It's all yours," I tell him. "I'll stick to this samo-thing."

"Samosa," the mixed-breed repeats. He gobbles up the spicy chicken and smiles. "Thanks . . . um . . . what's your name?"

"Sparky," I tell him.

"I'm Raj," the mixed-breed tells me. "Pleased to meet you. You're not from around here, are you?"

"No," I say. "I don't even know where *here* is."

"You're in Agra, India," Raj tells

me. "A very magical city. You'll see things here you won't see anywhere else in the world. At least that's what I hear. I've never actually *been* anywhere else."

I've been lots of places. But I don't tell Raj that.

I don't want to have to tell him about my magic bone. He tried to get the lamp away from me. He might try to take my bone, too.

I take another bite of the samosa.

"You want me to show you around?" Raj asks.

I think about that. I have two more wishes left. One of them will take me home.

I could go home right now.

But that doesn't seem fair to my

new friend. I wouldn't have even known about the jinni in the lamp if he hadn't told me.

I think I should share another wish with him.

But just *one* more.

Because that third wish is all for me. It's the wish that will take me home.

CHAPTER 13

"See? Isn't that beautiful?" Raj asks me after we've been walking for a while.

I don't know what he is talking about.

My new friend and I stop to look around. All I see are legs. *Two-leg* legs. They're everywhere.

"Look up," Raj tells me.

I look up. There's a huge white building with a big round roof in front of us.

"Who lives there?" I ask Raj. "Do

you think they like dogs? Because it's hot out here. Maybe we could go inside, get some water, and—"

"Nobody lives in the Taj Mahal," Raj says, interrupting me.

"The Taj Ma-who?" I ask him.

"Taj Mahal," Raj says. "It means 'crown of palaces.'"

"Oh, it's a palace," I say. "I've seen a palace before. When I was in London. A queen lives in *that* palace. Not Queenie: That's a cat in my neighborhood."

Raj looks at me strangely. I can tell he has no idea what I'm talking about.

"Anyway," Raj says finally. "No one lives in the Taj Mahal. But two-legs come from far away to visit it."

I wonder if those two-legs use a magic bone or a magic lamp to bring them here.

"Does *your* two-leg visit the Taj Mahal a lot?" I ask Raj.

"I don't have a two-leg," Raj says.

He does not sound happy or sad. But I think it would be sad to live without a two-leg.

Still, Rehema and the other African wild dogs are happy. And they don't have any two-legs.

I guess it's different for every dog.

"Do you have a big pack of dogs that you live with?" I ask Raj.

"Nope," Raj says. "It's just me. Which is okay. At least I don't have to share my food with anyone."

I look down at the ground. That

doesn't sound like something a friend should say.

"But I'll share with *you*," Raj adds quickly. He smiles. "It's kind of nice having a friend. It can get pretty lonely for a stray dog around here."

Poor Raj. I know what it's like to be lonely. I feel that way whenever Josh goes away in his big metal machine with the four round paws.

But at least I know he's coming back.

Raj has no one coming back to him. He's all alone.

I bet if he had found the lamp, he would have wished for a *furever* friend.

I won't be in Agra forever. But as long as I am here, maybe I can do something nice for him.

"Are you still hungry?" I ask Raj. "Because if you are, I could wi—"

"Don't wish for the jinni to give us more food," Raj warns, interrupting me. "We should save our wishes for something really important. We only have two more."

I don't say anything, since I know that one of those wishes is for me only. That's the one that will take me home.

"Besides, we don't need a wish to get us some food," Raj says. "Two-legs around here drop their food all the time."

Sniffety, sniff, sniff.

Just then, my nose starts sniffing something sweet.

Sniffety, sniff, sniff.

And it smells nearby.

My paws start bouncing up and down. They must smell the sweet stuff, too. Which is weird, because paws don't have noses.

Before I know what is happening, my paws start running in the direction of the sweet smell.

Fast. Faster. *Fastest.*

But they can't go very fast in this big crowd of legs.

Just then I see a little two-leg. She is holding something in her paw and licking it.

The little two-leg smiles as she licks.

Sniffety, sniff, sniff.

That smells so *yummy, yum, yum.*

I drop my lamp by my front paws. Then I bark, "Can I have a lick of that sweet-smelling stuff?"

The little two-leg's eyes open wide. A big blob of the sweet-smelling stuff falls out of her paws.

"Thanks, little two-leg!" I bark. Then I start licking the sweet-smelling stuff.

Yummy, yum, yum. This is so cold and creamy.

Lick. Lick. Lick.
Yummy, yum—

Uh-oh!

Suddenly, I hear a lot of yelling. I don't know what the two-legs are saying. But they do not sound happy.

A two-leg lunges at me. He is shouting angrily.

Gulp! I wonder if that two-leg is a dogcatcher. I wonder if he wants to put me in a pound. I do not want to go to the pound. If I do, I may never get out.

I may never see Josh again!

"We gotta get out of here," Raj calls from somewhere in the crowd of angry two-legs.

He does not have to tell me twice.

My paws start bouncing. They begin to move.

"Don't forget the lamp!" Raj barks to me.

Oh right. The magic lamp. I scoop it up in my teeth.

"Follow me!" Raj barks.

Raj's paws are moving as fast as they can.

So *my* paws move as fast as they can.

"That's it, paws!" I shout to them. "Follow that tail!"

CHAPTER 14

"I don't understand two-legs," Raj says. "All they do is yell."

We have run a long way. Now we are sitting on the ground, watching two-legs walk all around us.

"Not every two-leg," I tell Raj. "Josh hardly ever yells."

"Who's Josh?" Raj asks me.

"My two-leg," I tell him.

Raj looks surprised. I guess it's because I never told him that I have a two-leg.

"What's your two-leg like?" he asks me.

"He's really nice," I say. "He feeds me. And he plays with me."

"I've never seen any two-leg act like that," Raj says. "All the two-legs here do is shoo me away."

"That's because none of those two-legs are your *special* two-leg," I tell him. "When you have a special two-leg, you are a team. A pack. You do things together."

"It might be nice to have a two-leg," Raj says slowly. "Then I wouldn't ever be lonely. But only if the right two-leg comes along."

"Oh yes," I agree. "It has to be the right two-leg. A two-leg you can love, and who will love you back."

"How do you know if you've found the right two-leg?" Raj wonders.

"You just know," I tell him. "When Josh pets my head or scratches me under the chin, it feels right. It makes my tail wag."

Ook! Ook! Ook!

Just then, I look up and see a group of four-legs on a wall.

At least I think they are four-legs. They look a little like two-legs, but they are covered in fur. And they have long tails.

Ook! Ook! Ook!

They make some weird noises, too.

What kind of a strange place has my new friend led me to now?

"Those monkeys are hilarious, aren't they?" Raj asks me.

I look up at the four-legs on the wall. Now I know what those four-legs are. They're monkeys!

I should have guessed. They look a little like the howler monkey I met when my magic bone took me to the Amazon Rain Forest.

Except *that* monkey howled really, really loudly. And *these* monkeys . . .

Ook! Ook! Ook!

These monkeys say *ook*.

The monkeys leap off the wall and

onto a nearby tree branch. A group of two-legs clap their paws.

"The two-legs love coming to the Agra Fort to see the monkeys," Raj says. "I don't blame them. They are pretty funny."

One of the monkeys jumps back to the wall. He twirls around in a circle.

The two-legs clap their paws. They smile and make that *ha-ha-ha* noise Josh sometimes makes when he is happy.

"I don't see what's so great about that," I say. "Any dog can twirl around in a circle."

To prove it, I leap up on my hind legs. Then I twirl in a circle.

"Hey, that's pretty good," Raj tells me.

The monkey on the wall looks at me. He opens his mouth wide.

Ook! Ook! Ook!

I have no idea what he is saying.

"Do you know any other tricks?" I bark to the monkey.

He doesn't answer me. Probably because he doesn't speak dog.

I try another trick. I lie down on my belly. Then I roll over. Then I sit up again.

A few of the two-legs look in my direction. Some of them clap their paws.

I smile at them. I like making two-legs happy.

"Hey, those tricks look like fun, Sparky," Raj says. "Can you show me how to twirl?"

"Sure!" I say. "Just do what I do."

Raj watches as I stand on my hind legs.

Then he stands on his hind legs.

I twirl in a circle.

Raj twirls in a circle.

More two-legs turn to look at us.

They clap their paws.

Ook! Ook! OOOOKKKK!

Those monkeys do not sound happy.

I don't think they like that the two-legs are smiling and clapping their paws for us.

The monkeys tap their heads. They dance around on the tree branch.

One of them hangs upside down by his tail.

The two-legs like that. They clap their paws, smile, and make more *ha-ha-ha* noises.

I cannot hang by my tail. My tail is not long or strong enough.

"No fair, monkeys!" I bark.

Whoosh! Plop!

One of the monkeys throws something right at me.

"What is that?" I ask Raj. "Is it food?"

Raj sniffs at the stuff the monkey threw.

"No. It's not food," he says.

"Then what is it?" I ask.

"It's monkey poop," Raj tells me.

Huh? "The monkeys are throwing poop at us?" I ask.

Raj nods.

"That's not nice!" I shout up to the monkeys in the tree.

The monkeys do not answer. Instead they throw more poop in my direction.

It feels like it's raining poop.

I do not like this at all.

Neither do the two-legs. They are not smiling, or clapping their

paws, or making that *ha-ha-ha* noise anymore.

Instead they look angry. A few of them start to shout.

I bet they are telling those monkeys to stop throwing their poop.

Wait a minute. *Wiggle, waggle, what's going on here?*

The two-legs are not shouting at the monkeys.

They are looking right at Raj and me.

"Don't be angry with us, two-legs," I say. "We're not the ones throwing poop."

But the two-legs don't understand. And I don't think they want us around here anymore.

Ook! Ook! Ook!

Plop. Plop. Plop.

Hey! That piece of monkey poop almost got me!

"I'm getting out of here!" Raj says.

"Right behind you," I say as I pick up the magic lamp.

Ook! Ook! Ook!

Plop!

This is *no* place for a dog.

CHAPTER 15

Raj and I run *up, up, up* to the top of a hill.

There are no two-legs up here. They are all walking on the road below.

I am glad to be away from all the crowds.

Raj opens his mouth to say something to me. But all I hear is—

Grumble rumble.

That's not Raj's mouth talking. It's his tummy. It's hungry.

Rumble grumble.

That's my tummy talking. It's hungry, too.

"Sounds like we need to walk back to the marketplace and find food," Raj says.

Food sounds really, really good. But walking doesn't. My paws are tired.

"That would be great," I say. "I just wish someone could carry me there."

"Sparky!" Raj shouts nervously. "You just used up another of our wishes!"

Just then, two big cows come walking by, below the hill.

"There's our ride," Raj says to me. "Boy, does that jinni work fast."

Raj jumps off the hill and lands right on the back of one of the cows.

The cow looks up. She sure is surprised.

But she doesn't shake Raj off. She just keeps walking.

Now that my wish has come true, I may as well go for a ride, too. I jump off the hill and land right on the back of the other cow.

"It's nice not to have to walk," Raj tells me as the cows head down the road. "But you better be careful with that last wish. Make it a good one."

I know exactly what I am going to do with my last wish. But I can't tell Raj. I have to get back to my magic bone first.

Sniffety, sniff, sniff. I smell food everywhere. My magic bone, and my last wish, can wait. Food first!

Raj sticks his nose up in the air. "Mmmm. I smell lamb tandoori," he says.

"Is that food?" I ask him.

"Yup." Raj smiles. "It's the best. Not too spicy. But oh so tasty."

"Sounds *yummy, yum, yum*," I say.

Raj sniffs again. "It's coming from down that small street," he says. "Right around the corner from the

Mankameshwar Temple."

I look over at a building near the side of the road. I know that place.

That's where I found my magic lamp.

"Come on," Raj says as he jumps off the back of his cow. "Maybe someone has dropped a few good pieces of lamb tandoori."

I jump off the back of my cow, too.

Wham! I land hard on the dusty road. Ouch!

"Thanks for the ride," I say as the cow walks off. Then I follow Raj down the crowded street.

"Are there always so many two-legs here?" I ask Raj.

"The marketplace is always busy," Raj says as we dart among all the two-legs. "Don't stop walking. These crowds will stomp right on you if you do."

I think Raj is right. The two-legs are all walking very fast. They don't even notice that there are two little dogs walking near their paws.

Hey! *Wiggle, waggle, what's that?*

Up ahead I see a small two-leg. One of his legs is all wrapped up in something white. He has two big sticks under his arms.

"What's that little two-leg doing?" I ask Raj. "Why is his leg all wrapped up?"

"I've seen that before," Raj says. "The bone inside his leg is broken. The wooden sticks help him walk until his bone is fixed."

I watch how the small two-leg leans on his long wooden sticks every time he takes a step. He is moving very slowly.

Suddenly, the little two-leg loses his grip on one of the sticks. He falls to the ground with a *THUD*.

"That had to hurt," Raj says.

I hear a loud noise coming from behind us. I turn around. There's a big crowd of two-legs walking this way.

There are so many of them. They are taking up the whole street. It looks like the big crowd of wildebeests I saw moving through the Serengeti. Except these are two-legs.

The two-legs are busy talking to one another.

Some are looking at the buildings on either side.

They do not seem to notice the hurt two-leg lying in the middle of the road.

I'm afraid one of them will step on the two-leg's hurt leg. The same way someone stepped on my paw when I first got here.

"Get up, little two-leg!" I bark loudly. "You have to get up. *Now!*"

The little two-leg spots the big crowd of people coming toward him. He grabs one of his sticks. He stretches and tries to get the other stick. But it has fallen too far away.

He can't stand up. Not without that other stick to help him.

The little two-leg is shouting something. He sounds scared.

Now I hear someone else shouting over the crowd. She sounds scared, too.

I wonder if she is trying to call out to the little two-leg.

The little two-leg with the hurt leg bone starts crawling on the ground. He is trying to get to the other stick before the big crowd tramples him.

I have to do something. But what?

Suddenly, I remember the magic lamp that is clenched between my teeth. I still have one wish left.

But if I use my wish to help the little two-leg, I can't use it to get back to Josh.

And if my magic bone is still broken, I may be stuck here in Agra. Or wind up somewhere else.

Somewhere that isn't my home.

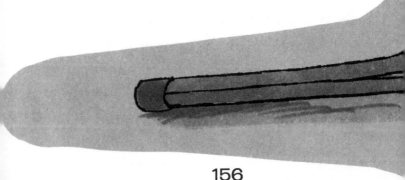

I look behind me. The crowd of two-legs is getting closer.

I look in front of me. The two-leg with the broken bone is still crawling on the ground, trying to reach his other stick.

"I wish the bone would be fixed!" The words are out of my mouth before I can stop them.

I know I have done the right thing. I cannot let that little two-leg get trampled. He has to get up and get out of the way.

He needs the jinni's help more than I do.

I can feel the big crowd of people getting closer and closer. Then, suddenly, out of nowhere, Raj darts in front of the crowd.

He's got something in his mouth.
It's the little two-leg's other stick!

Raj drags the long stick over to
the two-leg. The two-leg takes it in
his paw. Then he uses his two sticks
and stands up.

Slowly, he makes his way to the side of the road. He has water raining from his eyes.

The little two-leg is looking in the crowd. I think he is trying to find someone.

More and more two-legs go by. But the little two-leg does not seem to see the one he is looking for.

Still, at least he's not alone.

Raj is by his side.

"Stay away from this two-leg," Raj barks at the crowd.

Just then, a big two-leg hurries over to the little hurt two-leg.

She has water raining from her eyes, too. But she is smiling.

I watch as the big two-leg wraps her paws around the little two-leg.

Then she bends down and pets Raj on the head.

Raj's tail wags—a little.

Raj raises his head. The little two-leg scratches under his chin.

Raj's tail wags harder. Much, much harder.

Just the way my tail wags when Josh scratches under my chin.

"Hey, Sparky!" Raj shouts in my direction. "I think I found the right ones!"

I am happy for Raj. My tail must be happy, too, because it starts to wag.

The big two-leg says something to the little one.

The little two-leg smiles.

Then the big one scoops up Raj in her paws. She starts to walk away.

"What's going on?" Raj barks loudly.

"I think she's taking you home," I bark to Raj.

Raj's tail wags harder. "*Home*," he says. "I like the way that sounds. Do you want to come with us?"

I shake my head. "No, thanks," I shout to him. "I have my own two-leg to love."

As Raj walks away with his new pack, I can feel the magic lamp between my teeth. Only it's not magic anymore. *There are no more wishes left.*

CHAPTER 16

My stomach is feeling all flippy and floppy.

My legs are shaky.

My tail is tucked between my legs.

I'm scared. What if I dig up my magic bone and it doesn't work?

What if I wind up somewhere else that isn't home?

What if I can't *ever* get home again?

What if I never see my Josh again?

No. I can't let that happen. I have to dig up my bone. I have to take a bite. And my bone has to *kaboom* me home.

It just has to.

I go over to the small patch of grass near a little tree at the side of the road. It's the place where I buried my bone.

I take a deep breath. And then I start to *diggety, dig, dig.*

Dirt flies all over the place.

Diggety, dig, dig. Diggety, dig— There it is! My magic bone. It's right where I left it.

I look at my bone. I don't see the crack anymore. MY BONE IS FIXED!

But how? I used my last wish to help the little two-leg with the broken bone.

But maybe his bone isn't really fixed. Maybe he was just able to get up on his own.

Maybe the jinni fixed *my* bone instead.

Yes! That's it! It has to be.

This time I remember my manners. "Thank you, invisible jinni!" I shout.

Sniffity, sniff, sniff. My bone smells delicious. It's sooo meaty. I just have to take a bite.

Which means I have to let go of my magic lamp.

But I like the lamp, even if there are no wishes left.

It's still a great chew toy.

So I hold my lamp between my paws.

Then I bend down and grab the bone between my teeth.

CHOMP! I take a big bite of my magic bone.

Wiggle, waggle, whew. I feel dizzy—like my insides are spinning all around—but my outsides are standing still. Stars are twinkling in front of my eyes—even though it's daytime! All around me I smell food—fried chicken, salmon, roast beef. But there isn't any food in sight.

Kaboom! Kaboom! Kaboom!

There's my tree!
And my fence!

And my house!

I am home. Right where I belong.

Hooray for my magic bone!

I run over to where Josh grows his flowers, and I start to dig.

Diggety, dig, dig.

Dirt flies all over the place. *Diggety, dig, dig.*

I have made a great big hole. I drop

my bone into the hole and *pushity, push, push* the dirt back.

My bone is buried deep in the dirt. No one can find it. Except me, of course.

HISS!

I hear a loud noise coming from high up in my tree.

MEOW!

I look up. I see Queenie. She is sitting on a branch and glaring at me. But I'm not afraid.

"Go away, Queenie!" I bark angrily at her. "I've scared away much fiercer cats than you!"

HISS!

Queenie sounds mad. But she leaps off the tree branch, onto my fence, and into the next yard.

Yay! I win.

Vroom. Vroom.

I hear something coming from in front of our house. It sounds like Josh's metal machine with the big round paws.

Josh is home! I got back just in time.

Click. That's the sound of our gate opening.

I look up. *There he is.* It's Josh.

"Josh! Josh! Josh!" I bark as I race over to him. "I'm home! You're home! We are home together!"

Josh smiles and pets my head. I love when Josh pets my head.

Then he looks down at the ground. He gets a funny look on his face. He picks up my magic lamp.

Josh looks at the lamp. Then he looks at me. Then he looks at the lamp again.

I wish I could tell Josh all about the jinni that used to live in that lamp.

And about Raj and the monkeys who throw poop.

And about Rehema and the African wild dogs.

And the mean giant cats.

But I can't. Because I don't speak two-leg. And Josh doesn't speak dog.

So instead, I just rub against Josh's leg. I smile up at him. I am telling Josh that I am glad that he and I are in the same pack.

Josh smiles back at me. He pets my head.

I do not need to speak two-leg to understand that.

I can tell he feels the same way.

Fun Facts about Sparky's Visits to the Serengeti and Agra, India

The Serengeti

The Serengeti National Park is located in east central Africa. It spreads all the way from northern Tanzania to southwestern Kenya. Animal preserves in the Serengeti were created to help protect the animals that live there. For example, at one time there weren't many lions in the Serengeti because so many had been killed by hunters. Today more than three thousand lions live there! The park is also working hard to keep other endangered animals safe from hunters, including wild dogs, elephants, cheetahs, and black rhinos.

Mount Kilimanjaro

Tanzania's Mount Kilimanjaro is the tallest mountain in all of Africa. It was formed millions of years ago, when three volcanoes began erupting. Mount Kilimanjaro is made up of hardened volcanic ash and lava. Today, two of the three volcanoes are extinct, which means they will never erupt again. But the third volcano is only dormant. That means that it could erupt some day. The last volcanic eruption on Mount Kilimanjaro happened more than two hundred years ago.

K = Kenya   T = Tanzania

The Migration of the Wildebeests

Each year more than two million animals travel out of the Tanzania part of the Serengeti National Park in a large group. They are searching for greener pastures in nearby Kenya. More than one and a half million wildebeests migrate each year. They are joined in the migration by about two hundred thousand zebras and five hundred thousand gazelles.

Rock Gongs

A rock gong is a large boulder that makes a loud, metallic noise when hit by a smaller rock. In ancient times, the Masai tribe of Tanzania used rock gongs to send messages to one another.

Hippos

Hippos may not eat meat, but that does not mean they are harmless. In fact, they can be quite dangerous if they are bothered. Hippos have sharp teeth and weigh up to nine thousand pounds. If they feel threatened, they will run toward the water, mowing down anyone who gets in their way.

The Legend of the Jinn

Even though they are just make-believe, stories about jinn have been found in folktales from India and Arabia since ancient times. In many of the stories, jinn are able to grant wishes to the people who free them.

Mankameshwar Temple

This is one of the oldest religious sites in Agra, India. People line up to pray in the temple because legend has it that those who visit Mankameshwar Temple will have their wishes granted.

The Agra Fort

Built almost one thousand years ago, the Agra Fort is more like a small walled city than a fort. It is filled with beautiful marble carvings, brightly colored tile mosaic artwork, and huge stone statues. The Indian military still uses the northern part of the fort, so visitors are not allowed there. But the rest is open to visitors. Many come to see the monkeys who have made their home in the fort.

The Taj Mahal

This famous building was constructed more than three hundred years ago. It is made of white marble and other materials, and took more than twenty years to build. The Taj Mahal was built as a burial site for Mumtaz Mahal, the third wife of emperor Shah Jahan. Millions of visitors travel from all over each year to visit the Taj Mahal, making it one of the most popular tourist attractions not only in India, but in the world.

About the Author

Nancy Krulik is the author of more than two hundred books for children and young adults, including three *New York Times* Best Sellers. She is best known for being the author and creator of several successful book series for children, including Katie Kazoo, Switcheroo; How I Survived Middle School; and George Brown, Class Clown. Nancy lives in Manhattan with her husband, composer Daniel Burwasser, and her crazy beagle mix, Josie, who manages to drag her along on many exciting adventures without ever leaving Central Park.

About the Illustrator

You could fill a whole attic with Seb's drawings! His collection includes some very early pieces made when he was four—there is even a series of drawings he did at the movies in the dark! When he isn't doodling, he likes to make toys and sculptures, as well as bows and arrows for his two boys, Oscar and Leo, and their numerous friends. Seb is French and lives in England. His website is www.sebastienbraun.com.